Questions & Swords

Por mi voz habla la voz del Ejército Zapatista de Liberación Nacional.

Through my voice speaks the Zapatista Army for National Liberation.

FOLKTALES OF THE
ZAPATISTA REVOLUTION
As told by
Subcomandante
MARCOS

Questions & Swords

Illustrated by DOMITILA DOMÍNGUEZ
& ANTONIO RAMÍREZ
Essays by SIMON ORTIZ & ELENA PONIATOWSKA
Translations of Marcos' writing by DAVID ROMO

CINCO PUNTOS PRESS
EL PASO, TEXAS

MAKING THIS BOOK has been more like writing a poem or a novel than designing and publishing a book. During the whole process, we were talking to people and reading other books, our ideas changing and becoming more refined as we went along. Therefore, we want to thank all of those people who had a hand in putting this book together. First on our list are **Domi, Antonio** and the **Colectivo Callejero**. It has been a privilege to work with them on The Story of Colors / La Historia de los Colores and now on this project. **David Romo** translated "The Seventh Anniversary of the Zapista Uprising," "Story of Questions" and "The Story of the Sword, the Tree, the Stone & the Water," and served as our in-town consultant. Journalist **John Ross** was our Chiapas consultant. He was the one who suggested that we use the poem, "The Seventh Anniversary of the Zapista Uprising," at the beginning of the book to serve as introduction. His book The War against Oblivion: The Zapatista Chronicles (*Common Courage Press, 2000*) has been an invaluable daily resource. John, largely ignored by mainstream media, will long be remembered for giving U.S. readers a firsthand understanding of Marcos, the EZLN and the Mexican government's response to them. **Juana Ponce de Leon**,

Greg Ruggiero and **Dan Simon** at Seven Stories Press supported our project, and the Seven Stories selection of Marco's writings, Our Word is Our Weapon (*Seven Stories, 2000*) was on our desk for the last three months of this project. The community of small independent presses—working on similar projects in concert but chaordically—never ceases to amaze us. **Elena Poniatowska** and **Simon Ortiz** responded with enthusiasm to our request for essays. Believing the book important, they sat down and started writing. We are honored to have their words and ideas included here. Likewise **Aurora Camacho de Schmidt** and **Arthur Schmidt**, who translated Elena's article, did so on the normal small press deadline of "Hurry up! Hurry up!" **Ben Sáenz** gave us the idea to do the two books as one, thereby giving us elbow room to work. And thanks to the other folks here and everywhere—our always friend **Joe Hayes**, our New York volunteer **Rebekah Meola**, our forever smiling intern **Jonathan Gonzalez**, our book designer **Vicki Trego Hill**, who must always put up with our foolishness. Thanks also to the **supporters of the EZLN** we met in Guadalajara, from whom we purchased the photos of the Zapatista women and of Marcos.

And, once again, many thanks to the **Lannon Foundation** for funding this book and for their continued support.

Like John Ross before us, we want to dedicate this book to
LOS MUERTOS OF THE ZAPATISTA ARMY OF NATIONAL LIBERATION—Y LOS VIVOS.
May peace with honor and hope come to them and to the peoples they represent.

Printed in Hong Kong through Morris Press Limited.

Book and cover design and book production by Vicki Trego Hill of El Paso, Texas.

For more information, visit our website at **www.cincopuntos.com**
or call us at 1-800-566-9072 to receive a free catalog.

FIRST EDITION 10 9 8 7 6 5 4 3 2 1 Library of Congress Cataloging-in-Publication Data Marcos, subcomandante.
Questions and swords : folktales of the Zapatista revolution / by Subcomandante Marcos ; illustrated by Domitila Dominguez and Antonio Ramirez.— 1st ed.
p. cm. Folktales in English and Spanish. ISBN 0-938317-53-9 (pbk.) 1. Indians of Mexico—Mexico—Chiapas—Folklore. 2. Tales—Mexico—Chiapas.
3. Chiapas (Mexico)—History—Peasant Uprising, 1994- .—Folklore. F1219.1.C45 M37 2001 398.2'0972'7507—dc21 00-065716 CIP

contents

A Preface: January 1, 2001   pages 6 & 7

The Story of Questions   page 8
    as told by Subcomandante Marcos
    illustrated by Antonio Ramírez

Haah-ah, mah-eemah
Yes, it's the very truth   page 50
    essay by Simon Ortiz

**The Story of the Sword, the Tree, the Stone,
& the Water**   page 60
    as told by Subcomandante Marcos
    illustrated by Domitila Domínguez

Can a book explode like a bomb?   page 100
    essay by Elena Poniatowska

El Colectivo Callejero   page 109
Notes   page 112

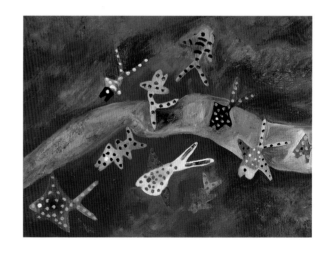

PHOTO COURTESY EZLN

JANUARY 1, 2001

EXACTLY SEVEN YEARS BEFORE THIS DATE *the Zapatista Army for National Liberation slipped out of the darkness of the Lancondon jungle and declared war against the Mexican government.*

The EZLN was, and is, a ragtag army of Mayan native people, courageous men and women who have chosen to pick up weapons and fight a war which—if numbers and weaponry be the only measures to foretell success and failure—they are destined to lose. They call their war la Guerra contra el olvido, *The War against Oblivion. They fight to retrieve and protect their land, and to preserve their culture and their language. They understood from the beginning that their enemy was not only the Mexican government, but also the "New World Economy," so they timed their rebellion to coincide with the first day of NAFTA, the North American Free Trade Agreement.*

From that first day seven years ago, one man—Subcomandante Marcos, or "el Sup"—became the media spokesman for the EZLN. A green-eyed meztizo, without a personal history, masked, mysterious, charismatic in language and style, he also became an international revolutionary and pop-culture hero. The media flocked to him. But in the midst of all the attention, he has stressed that the rebellion belongs to the Mayan people, that he is only "un subcomandante," and that—

Por mi voz habla la voz del Ejército Zapatista de Liberación Nacional.
Through my voice speaks the Zapatista Army for National Liberation.

Séptimo aniversario del alzamiento Zapatista
Seventh Anniversary of the Zapatista Uprising

HERMANOS Y HERMANAS INDÍGENAS MEXICANOS;

Hermanos y hermanas de México y el Mundo:

En este el año siete de la guerra contra el olvido, repetimos lo que somos.

Somos viento, nosotros. No el pecho que nos sopla.

Somos palabra, nosotros. No los labios que nos hablan.

Somos paso, nosotros. No el pie que nos anda.

Somos latido, nosotros. No el corazón que lo pulsa.

Somos puente, nosotros. No los suelos que se unen.

Somos camino, nosotros. No el punto de llegada ni de partida.

Somos lugar, nosotros. No quien lo ocupa.

No existimos, nosotros. Sólo somos.

Siete veces somos. Nosotros siete veces

Nosotros, el espejo repetido.

El reflejo, nosotros

La mano que apenas abre la ventana, nosotros

Nosotros, el mundo llamado a la puerta del mañana.

—COMANDANTE DAVID
& SUBCOMANDANTE MARCOS

INDIGENOUS BROTHERS AND SISTERS OF MEXICO;

Brothers and sisters of Mexico and the world:

In this, the seventh year of the war against oblivion, we repeat who we are.

We are wind, we are. Not the breast that breathes for us.

We are word, we are. Not the lips which speak to us.

We are steps, we are. Not the foot that moves us.

We are heartbeat, we are. Not the heart that pulses.

We are a bridge, we are. Not the lands that form a union.

We are road, we are. Not the point of arrival or departure.

We are place, we are. Not those who occupy that place.

We do not exist, we are. We only are.

Seven times we are. Seven times we are.

We are the reflection repeated.

The reflection, we are

The hand that just opened the window, we are,

We are the timid knock at the door of tomorrow.

—COMANDANTE DAVID
& SUBCOMANDANTE MARCOS

La Historia de las Preguntas

The Story of Questions

As told by
SUBCOMANDANTE
MARCOS

Illustrated by
ANTONIO RAMÍREZ

DE COMUNICADO AL PUEBLO MÉXICO:
13 DECIEMBRE 1994

Aprieta el frío en esta sierra. Ana María y Mario me acompañan en esta exploración, 10 años antes del amanecer de enero. Los dos apenas se han incorporado a la guerrilla y a mí, entonces teniente de infantería me toca enseñarles lo que otros me enseñaron a mí: a vivir en la montaña.

---

[1] **FROM COMMUNIQUÉ**
TO THE MEXICAN PEOPLE:
DECEMBER 13, 1994 [2]

The cold is bone-chilling in these mountains. Ana Maria and Mario are with me on this expedition, 10 years before the dawn of January.[3] The two have just joined the guerrilla army, and I, then an infantry lieutenant, take my turn to teach them what others have taught me: to live in the mountains.

9

AYER TOPÉ AL VIEJO ANTONIO por vez primera.
Mentimos ambos. Él diciendo que andaba para ver su
milpa, yo diciendo que andaba de cacería. Los dos
sabíamos que mentíamos y sabíamos que lo sabíamos.
Dejé a Ana María siguiendo el rumbo de la exploración y
yo me volví a acercar al río para ver si, con el clisímetro,
podía ubicar en el mapa un cerro muy alto que tenia al
frente, y por topaba de nuevo al viejo Antonio. El ha de
haber pensado lo mismo porque se apareció por el lugar
del encuentro anterior.

Como ayer, el viejo Antonio se sienta en el suelo, se
recarga en un huapac de verde musgo, y empieza a forjar
un cigarro. Yo me siento frente a él y enciendo la pipa.
El viejo Antonio inicia:

—No andas de cacería. Yo respondo: "Y usted no anda
para su milpa". Algo me hace hablarle de usted, con
respeto, a este hombre de edad indefinida y rostro curtido
como la del cedro, a quien veo por segunda vez en mi vida.
El viejo Antonio sonríe y agrega: "He oído de ustedes.
En las cañadas dicen que son bandidos. En mi pueblo

YESTERDAY I RAN INTO OLD ANTONIO for the first time. We both lied—him saying he was on his way to see his field, and me saying I was out hunting. Both of us knew we were lying and we knew we knew it. I left Ana Maria following the directions of the expedition, and I went back to the river to see if, with a clisimeter, I could locate on the map a very high hill that was up ahead. And to see if I could bump into Old Antonio again. He must have been thinking the same thing because he appeared at the same place where I found him before.

Like the day before, Old Antonio is sitting on the ground, leaning up against a hump of green moss, and beginning to roll a cigarette. I sit down in front of him and light my pipe. Old Antonio begins: "You're not hunting."

I respond: "You're not walking to your field." Something makes me speak formally—in a respectful manner—to this man of indefinite age with a faced tanned like cedar bark who I am seeing for the second time in my life. Old Antonio smiles and adds: "I've heard of you people. In the canyons, they say you are thieves. In my village, they

están inquietos porque pueden andar por esos rumbos".

"Y usted, ¿cree que somos bandidos?", pregunto. El
viejo Antonio suelta una gran voluta de humo, tose y
meg'a la cabeza. Yo me animo y le hago otra pregunta:
"¿Y quién cree usted que somos?"

"Prefiero que tú me lo digas", responde el viejo Antonio
y se me queda viendo a los ojos.

"Es una historia muy larga", digo y empiezo a contar
de cuando Zapata y Villa y la revolución y la tierra y la
injusticia y el hambre y la ignorancia y la enfermedad y la
represión y todo. Y termino con un "y entonces nosotros
somos el Ejercito Zapatista de Liberación Nacional". Espero
alguna señal en el rostro del viejo Antonio que no ha
dejado de mirarme durante mi plática.

"Cuéntame mas de ese Zapata", dice después de humo
y tos. Yo empiezo con Anenecuilco, me sigo con el Plan de
Ayala, la campaña militar, la organización de los pueblos,
la traición de Chinameca. El viejo Antonio sigue
mirándome mientras termino el relato.

are worried because you are walking these trails."

"And you, do you believe that we are bandits?" I ask. Old Antonio exhales a long wisp of smoke, coughs, and shakes his head. I get up my courage and ask him another question. "So who do you think we are?"

"I'd rather you tell me," he says and looks me straight in the eyes.

"It's a long story," I say. And I begin to tell about the times of Zapata and Villa and the revolution and the land and the injustice and the hunger and the ignorance and the sickness and the repression and everything. And I finish with "and thus we are the Zapatista Army of National Liberation." I wait for some sign from Old Antonio who never stopped looking at me during my speech.

"Tell me more about that Zapata," he says after another puff and a cough. I begin with Anenecuilco, then I follow with the Plan de Ayala, the military campaign, the organization of the villages, the betrayal at Chinameca.[4] Old Antonio continues to stare at me until I finish.

"**NO ASÍ FUE**", me dice. Yo hago un gesto de sorpresa y solo alcanzó a balbucear: "¿No?"

"No", insiste el viejo Antonio. "Yo te voy a contar la verdadera historia del tal Zapata."

"**IT WASN'T LIKE THAT**" he tells me. I'm surprised and all I can do is mumble, "No?"

"No," insists old Antonio. "I'm going to tell you the real story of this so-called Zapata."

SACANDO TABACO Y "DOBLADOR", el viejo Antonio inicia su historia que une y confunde tiempos viejos y nuevos, tal y como se confunden y unen el humo de mi pipa y de su cigarro.

"Hace muchas historias, cuando los dioses más primeros, los que hicieron el mundo, estaban todavía dando vueltas por la noche, se habían dos dioses que eran el Ik'al y el Votán.

OLD ANTONIO TAKES OUT HIS TOBACCO and rolling paper and begins his story, a story where old and new events mix and get lost in each other, just as the smoke from his cigarette and my pipe mix and get lost in each other.

"Many stories ago, when the first gods—those who made the world were still circling through the night, there were these two other gods— Ik'al and Votán.

DOS eran de
uno sólo.
Volteándose el
uno se mostraba
el otro,
volteándose el
otro se mostraba
el uno. Eran
contrarios.

"**THE TWO** were only one. When one was turning himself around, the other one would show himself, and when the other one was turning himself around, the first one would show himself. They were opposites.

19

EL UNO LUZ ERA como mañana de mayo en el río.
El otro era oscuro, como noche de frío y cueva.

"ONE WAS LIGHT like a May morning at the river.
The other was dark like night of cold and cave.

ERAN LO MISMO.
Eran uno los dos,
porque el uno
hacía al otro. Pero
no se caminaban,
quedando se
estaban siempre
estos dos dioses
que uno eran
sin moverse.

"**THEY WERE** the same thing. They were one, these two, because one made the other. But they would not walk themselves, staying there always, these two gods who were one without moving.

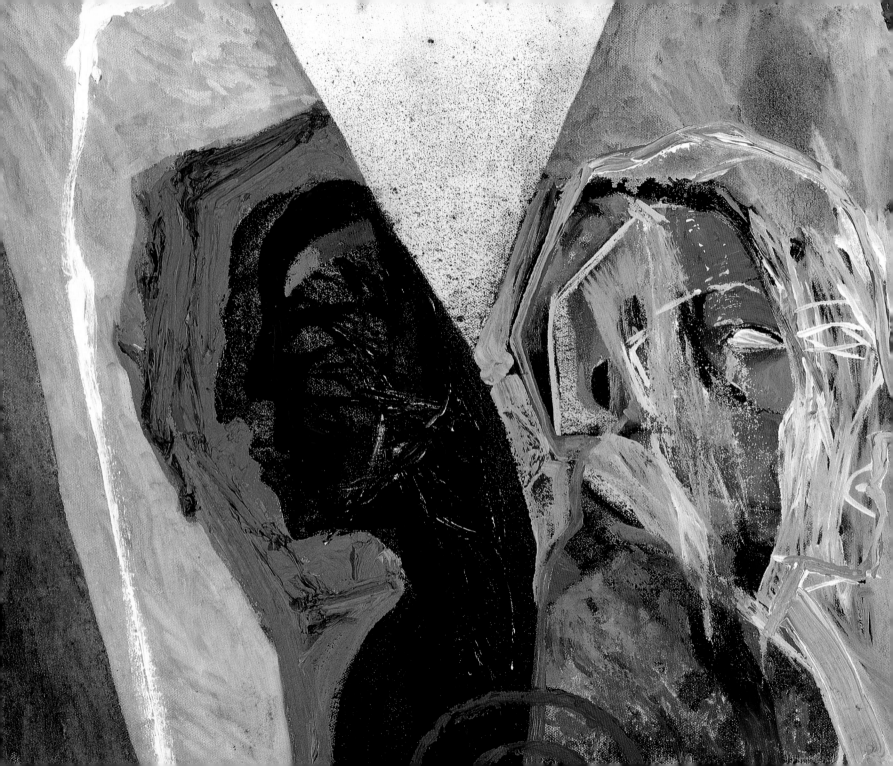

"**¿QUÉ HACEMOS PUES?**", preguntaron los dos.

"Está triste la vida así como estamos de por sí", tristeaban los dos que uno eran en su estarse.

"No pasa la noche", dijo el Ik'al.

"No pasa el día", dijo el Votán.

"'**WHAT SHOULD WE DO THEN?**' the two of them asked.

'Life is sad enough as it is,' they lamented, the two who were one in staying without moving.

'Night never passes,' said I'kal.

'Day never passes,' said Votán.

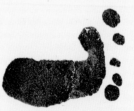

Through my voice speaks the Zapatista Army for National Liberation 25

"CAMINEMOS", dijo el uno que dos era.

"¿Cómo?", preguntó el otro.

"¿Para dónde?", preguntó el uno.

Y vieron que así se movieron tantito, primero para preguntar cómo, y luego para preguntar dónde. Contento se puso el uno que dos era cuando vio que tantito se movían. Quisieron los dos al mismo tiempo moverse y no se pudieron.

"'LET'S WALK,' said the one who was two.

'How?' asked the other.

'Where?' asked the one.

And they saw that they had moved a little, first to ask how, then to ask where. The one who was two became very happy when the one saw that they were moving themselves a little. Both of them wanted to move at the same time, but they couldn't do it to themselves.

"¿CÓMO HACEMOS PUES?"

Y se asomaba primero el uno y luego el otro y se movieron otro tantito y se dieron cuenta que si uno primero y otro después entonces sí se movían y sacaron acuerdo que para moverse primero se mueve el uno y luego se mueve el otro y empezaron a moverse y nadie se acuerda quién primero se movió para empezar a moverse porque muy contentos estaban que ya se movían...

"'HOW SHOULD WE DO IT THEN?'

And one would come around first and then the other and they would move just a little bit more and they realized that they could move if one went first, then the other. So they came to an agreement that—in order to move—one had to move first, then the other. So they started walking and now no one remembers who started walking first because at the time they were so happy just to be moving...

Through my voice speaks the Zapatista Army for National Liberation

...Y "¿QUÉ IMPORTA QUIÉN PRIMERO si ya nos movemos?", decían los dos dioses que el mismo eran y se reían y el primer acuerdo que sacaron fue hacer baile y se bailaron, un pasito el uno, un pasito el otro, y tardaron en el baile porque contentos estaban de que se habían encontrado. Ya luego se cansaron de tanto baile y vieron qué otra cosa pueden hacer...

"...AND 'WHO CARES WHO WAS FIRST since we're moving now?' said the gods who were one and the same and they laughed at each other and the first agreement they made was to dance, and they danced, one little step by one, one little step by the other, and they danced for a long time because they were so happy that they had found each other. Then they got tired of so much dancing and they looked for something else to do.

...Y LO VIERON que la primera pregunta de "¿cómo moverse?" trajo la respuesta de "juntos pero separados de acuerdo", y esa pregunta no mucho les importó porque cuando se dieron cuenta ya estaban moviéndose y entonces se vino la otra pregunta cuando se vieron que había dos caminos:

"AND THEY SAW that the first question was, 'How do we move?' and the answer was, 'Together but separately and in agreement.' But that question wasn't important anymore because they realized that they were already walking, and so another question came up when they saw that there were two roads in front of them:

EL UNO ESTABA MUY CORTITO y ahí nomás llegaba y claro se veía que ahí nomás cerquita se terminaba el camino ese y tanto era el gusto de caminar que tenían en sus pies que dijeron rápido que el camino que era cortito no muy lo querían caminar y sacaron acuerdo de caminarse el camino largo

---

"ONE ROAD WAS VERY SHORT and it just got over to *there* and they could see clearly that this road would end right away and their feet were so full of joy from walking that they said right then that the first road was too short and they didn't want to walk it and so they made an agreement to walk the long road.

Y YA SE IBAN A EMPEZAR A CAMINARSE, cuando la respuesta de escoger el camino largo les trajo otra pregunta de "¿a dónde lleva este camino?"; tardaron pensando la respuesta y los dos que eran uno de pronto llegó en su cabeza de que sólo si lo caminaban el camino largo iba a saber a dónde lleva porque así como estaban nunca iban a saber para dónde lleva el camino largo.

Y entonces se dijeron el uno que dos era:

"AND THEY WERE GOING TO START WALKING when their answer to choose the long road brought another question—'Where does this road take us?' They took a long time to think about the answer and the two who were one got the bright idea that only by walking the long road were they going to know where the road took them. If they remained where they were, they were never going to know where the long road leads.

The two who were one said to each other:

"**PUES VAMOS A CAMINARLO, PUES**" y lo empezaron a caminar, primero el uno y luego el otro. Y ahí nomás se dieron cuenta de que tomaba mucho tiempo caminar el camino largo y entonces se vino la otra pregunta de "¿cómo vamos a hacer para caminar mucho tiempo?" y quedaron pensando un buen rato y entonces el Ik'al clarito dijo que él no sabía caminar de día y el Votán dijo que él de noche miedo tenía de caminarse y quedaron llorando un buen rato

---

"'**SO LET'S WALK IT THEN,**' and they started walking, first the one and then the other. And only then and there did they realize that it was taking a long time to walk the long road, so another question came up: 'How are we going to walk for such a long time?' And they stayed thinking a good while and then Ik'al said real clearly that he didn't know how to walk by day and Votán said he was afraid to walk at night and they stayed there, crying for a long time.

Y YA LUEGO QUE ACABÓ LA CHILLADERA que se tenían se pusieron de acuerdo y lo vieron que el Ik'al bien que se podía caminar de noche y que el Votán bien que se podía caminar de día y que el Ik'al lo caminara al Votán en la noche y así sacaron la respuesta para caminarse todo el tiempo. Desde entonces los dioses caminan con preguntas y no paran nunca, nunca se llegan y se van nunca.

"AND WHEN ALL THE WAILING and hollering was over, they came to an agreement and they saw that it was fine for Ik'al to walk only at night and for Votán to walk only during the day and Ik'al would walk for Votán during the night and that is how they came up with the answer for walking all the time. Since then the gods have walked with questions and they never, never stop—they never arrive and they never go away.

Y ENTONCES ASÍ aprendieron los hombres y mujeres verdaderos que las preguntas sirven para caminar, no para quedarse parados así nomás. Y, desde entonces, los hombres y mujeres verdaderos para caminar preguntan, para llegar se despiden y para irse saludan. Nunca se están quietos.

"THIS IS HOW the true men and women learned that questions are for walking, not for just standing around and doing nothing. And since then, when true men and women want to walk, they ask questions. When they want to arrive, they take leave. And when they want to leave, they say hello. They are never still."

YO ME QUEDO MORDISQUEANDO la ya corta boquilla de la pipa esperando a que el viejo Antonio continúe pero él parece no tener ya la intención de hacerlo. Con el temor de romper algo muy serio pregunto: "¿Y Zapata?"

El viejo Antonio se sonríe: "Ya aprendiste que para saber y para caminar hay que preguntar".

Tose y enciende otro cigarro que no supe a qué hora lo forjó y, por entre el humo que sale de sus labios, caen las palabras como semillas en el suelo:

I'M LEFT GNAWING AND BITING at the short end of my pipe while I wait for old Antonio to go on with his story, but it seems he no longer has any intention of doing so. Afraid to interfere with something very serious, I ask, "And Zapata?"

Old Antonio smiles: "You've already learned that to know and to walk, you first have to ask."

He coughs and lights another cigarette that I didn't know he had rolled and amid the smoke that comes out of his lips, words fall like seeds to the ground:

"**EL TAL ZAPATA SE** apareció acá en las montañas.
No se nació, dicen. Se apareció así nomás. Dicen que es
el Ik'al y el Votán que hasta acá vinieron a parar en su
largo camino y que, para no espantar a las gentes buenas,
se hicieron uno sólo. Porque ya de mucho andar juntos,
el Ik'al y el Votán aprendieron que era lo mismo y que
podían hacerse uno sólo en el día y en la noche y
cuando se llegaron hasta acá se hicieron uno y se
pusieron de nombre Zapata…

"**THE ONE THEY CALL ZAPATA** appeared here in the
mountains. He wasn't born himself, they say. He just
appeared, just like that. They say he is the Ik'al and the
Votán who came here while they were on their long walk
and so that they wouldn't scare the good people, they
became one. Because after much walking together, Ik'al
and Votán discovered that they were one and the same
and that they could make themselves one during both
the day and night. When they got here they made themselves one and gave themselves the name of Zapata…

...Y DIJO EL ZAPATA que hasta aquí había llegado y acá iba a encontrar la respuesta de a dónde lleva el largo camino y dijo que en veces sería luz y en veces oscuridad, pero que era el mismo, el Votán Zapata y el Ik'al Zapata, el Zapata blanco y el Zapata negro, y que eran los dos el mismo camino para los hombres y mujeres verdaderos".

"...AND ZAPATA SAID that this is where he had arrived—where he was going to find where the long road led to and he said he would be light at times and other times darkness, but he was one and the same, the Votán Zapata and the Ik'al Zapata, the white Zapata and the black Zapata. And these two were both the same road for all true men and women to follow."

IT HAS BEEN MORE THAN FIVE HUNDRED YEARS. What shall happen? That is the question, not the only one but one of the first ones. And after more than five hundred years of loss of land and life, what shall be done? Those are questions Indian people of the Americas are asking.

That is how they live history.

"The Story of Questions" is about Zapata. But it is also not about Zapata. It is about what shall happen. It is about what shall be done.

Indian people know history is lived in the time and moment it is taking place. History is in the moment. History is not the past. Nor is it the future. And you ask questions so you will know history is taking place. You live history therefore.

And with our questions, that is the history we are living.

Haah-ah, mah-eemah
Yes, it's the very truth

by Simon Ortiz

FIVE HUNDRED YEARS and more ago, European people came to our Native homeland. And change, change, change happened. Much of the change has been destructive. And there has been loss, loss, loss. And more loss.

We have not known what to do with the loss. Since our knowledge of history is to live history, we have lived the loss. And when we live the loss, we live more loss.

We have to walk then. To move. To not be still. To not stay in the loss. And to not live in the loss. And to face the questions. What shall happen now? What shall be done?

A STORY IS MORE than just a story, I believe. That's the first thought that came to me when I learned of Viejo Antonio's stories—"The Story of Questions" and "The Story of the Sword, the Tree, the Stone, & the Water" as told by Subcomandante Marcos. Yes. Or *Haah-ah, mah-eemah* (Yes, it's the very truth) in the Keres language of the Acoma people from whom I come. Story is what we live. It is not just what we tell and it is not just what we hear. Story and the telling of story is what "living the story" is. I am certain Viejo Antonio would agree. *Haah-ah, mah-eemah.*

THE WAR FOR THE LAND, culture and community had been going on for a long time. For so long there was really no sense of time about it. No one seemed to know for certain when the war had begun. When it started that is. Nor when it would end.

It had been going on so long it felt like forever. Maybe it would never end. If no one knew when or for certain when it began, then it might never end. The war would just go on and on. Forever.

Why didn't anyone know how long it had been going on? Why didn't anyone know when it began way back when? *Meeshru maiqkuh hamah*, the people said. The elders of the people, that's what they said. Speaking in low soft matter-of-fact voices: *Meeshru maiqkuh hamah.* A very long time ago.

Just fact, a quiet softly spoken fact, nothing more than that. A recognition of something no one could say anything about, something no one could dispute.

The war had become a fact. A normal and ordinary fact of life.

IT SEEMS LIKE *we had been in a struggle for a long time. I don't remember a time when there was no struggle. There was always tension. I was afraid. I was worried. I felt like things were unpredictable. I could never tell what was going to happen next. Perhaps I even felt like I didn't know what was going to happen at any given moment. I could not tell what would happen next. It felt like a life and death matter. It was not a good feeling.*

WHEN NATIVE AMERICANS learned about the uprising in Chiapas in early January 1994, they knew it was time for the people to rise. To rise. To rise. It was good news! Although mostly it wasn't immediate news.

That is, people didn't hear about it right away. That is, people didn't hear about it at the same time nor all at once. And although most Native people didn't know exactly what to make of it, they knew something was going on.

Gradually though, and eventually, they learned about the Zapatista uprising. The mobilization of the Zapatista Army of National Liberation. The EZLN rebellion. The Mayan revolt.

It was almost like hearing gossip, a bit here, a bit there. Almost like it was only a rumor. And even though the news was welcome news, there was perhaps a kind of doubting also. Which had to do with the way colonized Indigenous people have gotten used to. Maybe it wasn't really taking place.

But something *was* taking place. And soon, even though people didn't know exactly what to make of it at first, it was good news!

But good news no one was sure about? Yes. Because it was the kind of news we had been waiting for. *Haa-ah kaimahtse*. Yes, it's true.

It was news we wanted to believe more than any kind of news.

Because it was news that was more than just news! *Kaimahtse*.

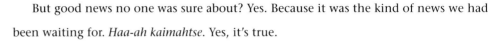

SINCE 1492, when European invasion of the continents of the Americas began with the arrival of Christopher Columbus, Indigenous people have tried to protect their land, culture, and community. Although the period of time since then has actually been just over 500 years, this is the "war" that has felt like forever. And this is the war Indigenous people (who are also called Indians, or Native Americans, or American Indians) have vainly wished would come to an end.

More recently, over the past four decades since the early 1960s, Indigenous people have struggled to assert themselves, particularly in defense against Americanization. And before that, during the 1920s and '30s, Natives fought the social, economic, and political forces arrayed against them by the federal, state, and corporate governments.

By the end of the 19th century, the prevalent U.S. belief was that "the Wild West," all of which was aboriginal Native homeland, had been won from the Indians. The Indian wars in the Americas were over, and the savage life of the savage Indians was over.

Now the savages were "being civilized" on Indian reservations. Now they were being assimilated and acculturated into American society. Now the Indian was no longer a culturally distinctive Indigenous entity.

That's why we were in a constant and often desperate struggle to assert ourselves as Native American people.

In effect it was a life and death struggle for our Native land, culture and community.

That's why when we heard about the uprising by the Indians of Chiapas it was good news. Even though we weren't entirely sure what was taking place and we didn't have much detail about what was happening, it was good news nonetheless.

Yes. No doubt about it, the news from the South was good news!

DESPITE THE U.S. CONSTITUTION'S RHETORIC about democracy and freedom of religion, the Sun Dance ceremonies of the Plains people's culture had been outlawed by federal fiat just like the Katzina ceremonies of the Pueblos had been banned as savage, heathen, and pagan. Nevertheless, Native religious ceremonies were sacred and holy. That's what the people said: Our religious ways are sacred and holy; they are the essence and form of our people's way; they cannot be anything but sacred and holy.

On many occasions in the early decades of the 20th century, Native Americans battled the U.S. Congress when laws were proposed to ban Indigenous religious practices. And they argued against federal proposals to allow non-Indian settlement upon Indigenous lands. Pueblo Indian religious events or ceremonies involving Katzina were eventually allowed to be practiced although they were virtually forced "underground"—becoming primarily private as cultural property—in order to keep them from being corrupted and culturally demeaned.

And non-Indian claims to Indian lands? For the most part, non-Indian claims were upheld in non-Indian courts of law. White settlers—actually squatters—and their descendants continued to remain securely on traditional Native homelands. Such as in

northern New Mexico, such as in the Black Hills of South Dakota. And even though many Native Americans opposed the Indian Reorganization Act of 1934 because it derogated traditional cultural governance, U.S. law now imposed federally sanctioned Bureau of Indian Affairs-styled governments on Native tribes.

By the mid-1930s during the New Deal era, Indigenous people of the United States were now essentially and categorically defined as "Indians" who were American citizens. Many felt they had become as "free" as other U.S. citizens, meaning, despite their on-going and determined resistance, Native Americans had become "Americanized" against their will.

Yes, the news from the South was welcome. And encouraging. And invigorating. Inspiring.

THE FISHING RIGHTS FIGHTS in the 1960s in Washington, Oregon, Nevada, California, and other places were grassroots, downhome struggles by Native people who depended upon fishing—and hunting and traditional farming also—as livelihood.

Fishing was food and income, and fishing was a cultural way of life. National Indian Youth Council (NIYC) youth, most of them reservation-raised college students then, were frontline activists and spokespeople for their elders, and they were determined to back the insistent stance of their parents and grandparents.

There is no other way to describe their determined position except to say it was Native American social, cultural, and political resistance. It was a necessary stance to take on behalf of their Indigenous and aboriginal right to be who they were as Native people. We are Indian! That's what Native activists said and stood for; that's what they expressed with their words and actions! Especially the American Indian Movement (AIM) which formed in the latter 1960s, inspired by NIYC's earlier decisive actions.

AIM-inspired events—which included the liberation of Wounded Knee, the Longest Walk, and the Trail of Broken Treaties in the 1970s resulting in the siege and sacking of the Bureau of Indian Affairs in Washington, D.C.— brought frontal notice to the U.S. American public that Indians were not to be regarded as docile American hostage citizens any longer!

Red Power! America is Indian Country! We Shall Endure! These were more than rhetorical slogans. The 1969 Indian occupation of Alcatraz Island, the site of a former U.S. federal prison where Indian resistance fighters had been imprisoned early in the 20th century, was a statement to the world. Willing to face a large contingent of police from local, state, and federal agencies, Indians traveled from all over the U.S. to make a stand at Alcatraz Island in San Francisco Bay.

It was clear that Indian people who traveled from all corners of the American Indigenous world were committed to unity and solidarity with each other for the sake of their land, culture, and community.

THE WORD FROM CHIAPAS in southern Mexico was from a distance not so far away after all. Native Americans across the United States passed word to each other from reservation to reservation, and from reservations to urban areas where many of them lived. And this word crossed northern borders to Canada and beyond. And recrossed borders southward to Mexico, Guatemala, Panama, and beyond. Back and forth, east and west, north and south, all around.

IN THE FIVE HUNDRED PLUS YEARS since European arrival in the Americas, many changes have taken place critically and traumatically affecting Indigenous land, culture, and community. About this there is no doubt. Yet at the same time there is also a sense of continual cultural on-going insisted upon by Indigenous people. It is an absolute sense of an Indigenous cultural community that involves the inter-related elements of the human, natural, and spiritual environment. That is what Indigenous cultural identity and wholeness is; this is the essence of Existence. Without this essence, life cannot go on.

After more than five hundred years of oppression caused by an aggressive European cultural, social, political, economic system, the long awaited signal from Chiapas is strong, clear, and certain. We Shall Endure. We Shall Continue. And this is what the Indigenous people of the United States and throughout the Americas of the Western Hemisphere relate to directly. Made by the Zapatista Army of National Liberation, this is the signal heard by Native North America. *Haa-ah duwah kaimahtse.* Yes, this is the truth.

WITHOUT A DOUBT, also, nervous governmental authorities of the U.S. and Mexico—and other nations in the Western Hemisphere—are aware of the impression and impact the Zapatistas are making, especially because of the primary reason for the uprising: Native opposition to NAFTA!

In 1993, the North American Free Trade Agreement (NAFTA) was debated not only across the U.S. and in the U.S. Congress but also in Canada and Mexico. Stable social and political conditions were needed to insure a vigorous and healthy economy and to enhance Congressional approval of NAFTA, a decision favored by transnational corporate-investor interests.

It was obvious to governmental and corporate authorities that you couldn't have an Indian uprising right in the midst of a major capitalistic venture like NAFTA! Especially if the uprising were to jeopardize the establishment and implementation of NAFTA. Think of all the millions of dollars of profits that would be lost! Think of all the wealth and power that would not be gained.

Think of it: What if Indians throughout the Americas rose in united force to seek the return of their land, culture, and community? Think of it!

—Simon J. Ortiz

SIMON J. ORTIZ, *considered by his peers as an elder among Native North American writers, is an Acoma Pueblo author of poetry, short fiction essays and a book-length verse narrative "Surviving Columbus," on which was based a 1992 television documentary broadcast by the Public Broadcasting System. Among his works are* The People Shall Continue, From Sand Creek, Woven Stone *and* After and Before the Lightning. *He is also the editor of the seminal collection of essays,* Speaking for the Generations, Native Writers on Writing.

La Historia de la Espada, el Árbol, la Piedra y el Agua

The Story of the Sword, the Tree, the Stone & the Water

As told by
SUBCOMANDANTE MARCOS

Illustrated by
DOMITILA DOMÍNGUEZ

**DE COMUNICADO AL PUEBLO MÉXICO:
29 SEPTIEMBRE 1995**

Una madrugada septembrina de lodo y lluvia
nos sorprendió aquel año en que el otro terremoto
derrumbaba la apatía y el encerrarse en sí mismo
de un país entonces llamado México. El Viejo
Antonio avivó el fuego de la campita en la que
nos refugiamos. Intentar secarnos era inútil,
el Viejo Antonio lo sabía.

[1]**FROM COMMUNIQUÉ TO THE
MEXICAN PEOPLE:
SEPTEMBER 29, 1995** [5]

A September dawn of mud and rain surprised us
that year in which another earthquake toppled
the apathy and isolation of a country that in those
times called itself Mexico.[6] Old Antonio lit the fire
of our little camp where we took refuge. Trying to
keep dry was useless, and Old Antonio knew it.

AL SECARSE, el lodo se volvía tierra rasposa que hería la piel y los recuerdos. El Viejo Antonio pensaba, como yo, no en el lodo que se emplastaba hasta en el cabello, sino en ahuyentar a los chaquistes y zancudos que festinaban nuestra húmeda llegada. A la ceremonia del fuego siguió la del tabaco y, entre el humo de uno y de otro iniciamos una plática sobre la guerra de independencia. El Viejo Antonio escuchaba y asentía con la mirada cuando mis palabras traían a Hidalgo, a Morelos, a Guerrero, a Mina, al Pipila, a los Galeana. Yo no repetía una historia aprendida ni recitaba una lección, trataba de reconstruir la soledad de esos hombres y mujeres y su empeño en seguir adelante no obstante la persecución y la calumnia que sufrían. No terminó, cuando platicaba la larga resistencia de la guerrilla de Vicente Guerrero en las montañas mexicanas el Viejo Antonio me interrumpió con un carraspeo de ésos con los que él anunciaba que una nueva maravilla se llegaba a sus labios, como se llegaba el calorcillo de la pipa humeante.

"Eso me recuerda algo", dijo el Viejo Antonio mientras soplaba para avivar el fuego y los recuerdos. Así, entre insurgentes pasados y presentes, entre el encuentro de humo y fuego, el Viejo Antonio descargó, como quien se libra de un pesado pero valioso bulto, palabras que contaban la historia de la espada, el árbol, la piedra y el agua.

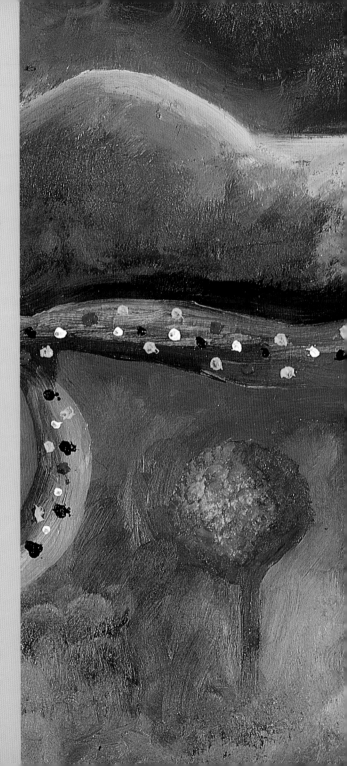

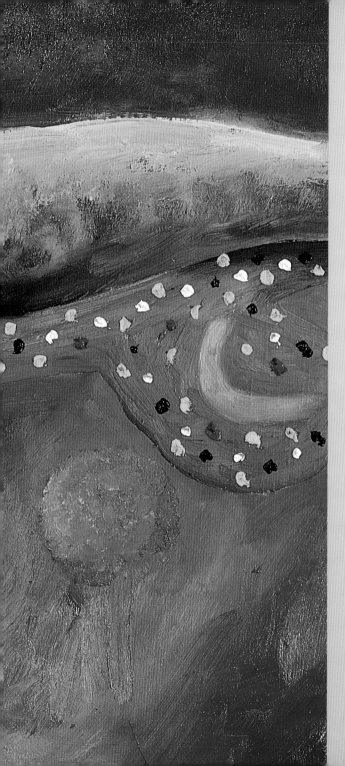

WHEN THE MUD DRIED, it became abrasive dirt that would scrape at our skin and memories. Old Antonio was thinking, like myself, not about the mud covering us from head to toe, but about scaring away the gnats and mosquitoes that feasted on our drenched arrival. The lighting of the fire followed the lighting of the tobacco and, between the smoke of the one and the other, we began to talk about the War of Independence.[7] Old Antonio was listening and nodding his head when my words came to Hidalgo, to Morelos, to Guerrero, to Mina, to Pipila, to los Galeana. I wasn't trying to repeat a story I had learned or recite a school lesson. I was trying to recall the loneliness of these men and women, their determination in going forward, regardless of the persecution and the slander that they suffered. My speech had not ended, but when I was describing the long resistance in the Mexican mountains by Vicente Guerrero's guerrilla army, Old Antonio stopped me by hawking up some phlegm in his throat, announcing that a new wonder had arrived at his lips, arriving just like the warmth from his smoking pipe.

"This reminds me of something," Old Antonio said while puffing away, trying to relight the fire and his memories. So, in the midst of revolutionaries past and present, in the space between smoke and fire, Old Antonio—like a man freeing himself of a heavy but valuable load—spewed out the words that told the story of the sword, the tree, the stone and the water.

MORDISQUEA LA PIPA el viejo Antonio. Mordisquea las palabras y les da forma y sentido. Habla el viejo Antonio, la lluvia se detiene a escuchar y el agua y la oscuridad dan un reposo.

"Nuestros más grandes abuelos tuvieron que enfrentar al extranjero que vino a conquistar estas tierras.

OLD ANTONIO IS CHEWING on his pipe. He's chewing at his words too, giving them form and meaning. Old Antonio speaks. The rain stops to listen, and the water and the darkness take a rest.

"Our grandparents from a long time ago had to confront the foreigner that came to conquer these lands.

VINO EL EXTRANJERO a ponernos otro modo, otra palabra, otra creencia, otro dios y otra justicia. Era su justicia sólo para tener él y despojarnos a nosotros.

Era su dios el oro. Era su creencia su superioridad. Era su palabra la mentira. Era su modo la crueldad. Los nuestros, los más grandes guerreros se enfrentaron a ellos, grandes peleas hubo entre los naturales de estas tierras para defender la tierra de la mano del extranjero.

"THE STRANGER CAME to impose a different way of life on us—a different way of talking, a different faith, different gods and different justice. It was only his justice that mattered to him and so he stripped us of ours.

"His god was gold. His faith was his superiority. His words were lies. His way of life was cruelty. Our heroes, the greatest warriors, confronted him. There were great battles between the peoples of these lands to defend the land against the hand of the stranger.

PERO GRANDE ERA TAMBIÉN la fuerza que traía la mano extraña. Grandes y buenos guerreros cayeron peleando y murieron. Las batallas seguían, pocos eran ya los guerreros y las mujeres y los niños tomaban las armas de los que caían.

Se reunieron entonces los más sabios de los abuelos y se contaron la historia de la espada, del árbol, de la piedra y el agua.

"BUT GREAT ALSO was the strength of the stranger's hand. Great and excellent warriors fell fighting and they died. The battles continued. Few were the warriors now, and so the women and the children took up the weapons of those that fell.

"The wisest of the grandfathers came together then and they told each other the story of the sword, the tree, the stone and the water.

Through my voice speaks the Zapatista Army for National Liberation   **69**

SE CONTARON que en los tiempos más viejos y allá en las montañas se reunieron las cosas que los hombres tenían para trabajarse y defenderse.

Andaban los dioses como era su modo de por sí, o sea que dormidos se estaban porque muy haraganes eran entonces los dioses que no eran los dioses más grandes, los que nacieron el mundo, los primeros.

"THEY TOLD EACH OTHER how in the oldest of times and there in the mountains men banded together to work and defend themselves.

"The gods were hanging around as was their usual habit. Or it could be they were sleeping, because they were really loafers, these gods, not like the greatest of gods, the ones that birthed the world, the first gods.

ESTABAN el hombre y la mujer gastándose en el cuerpo y creciendo en el corazón en un rincón de la madrugada. Silencio se estaba la noche. Callada se estaba porque ya sabía que muy poco le quedaba. Entonces habló la espada".

—Una espada así— se interrumpe el viejo Antonio y empuña un gran machete de dos filos. La luz del fuego arranca algunos destellos, un instante apenas, a la sombra luego. Sigue el viejo Antonio:

"IN A SMALL CORNER of the dawn, the man and the woman were exhausting each other's body and growing in their hearts. The night was being silence. It was quiet because it knew that only a little of itself remained. Then the sword spoke.

"A sword like this one"—Old Antonio interrupts himself and grabs a large double-edged machete in his fist. Sparks from the fire flicker a brief moment, then shadow. Old man Antonio continues:

"**ENTONCES HABLÓ LA ESPADA** y dijo:

—Yo soy la más fuerte y puedo destruirlos a todos. Mi filo corta y doy poder al que me toma y muerte al que me enfrenta.

—¡Mentira!— dijo el árbol. Yo soy el más fuerte, he resistido el viento y la más feroz tormenta. Se pelearon la espada y el árbol. Fuerte y duro se puso el árbol y enfrentó a la espada. La espada golpeó y golpeó hasta que fue cortando el tronco y derribó al árbol.

"THEN THE SWORD SPOKE and said, 'I am the strongest of all and I can destroy all of you. My blade cuts and I give power to those who hold me and death to those who confront me.'

"'That's a lie!' said the tree. 'I am the strongest. I have resisted the wind and the fiercest storm.' The sword and the tree fought each other. The tree made itself strong and hard and fought against the sword. The sword slashed and slashed at the trunk until it toppled the tree.

—**YO SOY LA MÁS FUERTE**— volvió a decir la espada.

—¡Mentira!— dijo la piedra. Yo soy la más fuerte porque soy dura y antigua, soy pesada y llena. Y se pelearon la espada y la piedra. Dura y firme se puso la piedra y enfrentó a la espada. La espada golpeó y golpeó y no pudo destruir a la piedra pero la partió en muchos pedazos. La espada quedó sin filo y la piedra muy pedaceada.

"'**I AM THE STRONGEST**,' the sword said again.

"'That's a lie!' said the stone. 'I am the strongest because I am hard and ancient. I am heavy and solid.' And so the sword and the stone fought. The stone made itself hard and dense and fought against the sword. The sword slashed and slashed and could not destroy the stone, but it broke the stone into many little pieces. The sword lost its sharpness, and the stone was scattered in pieces.

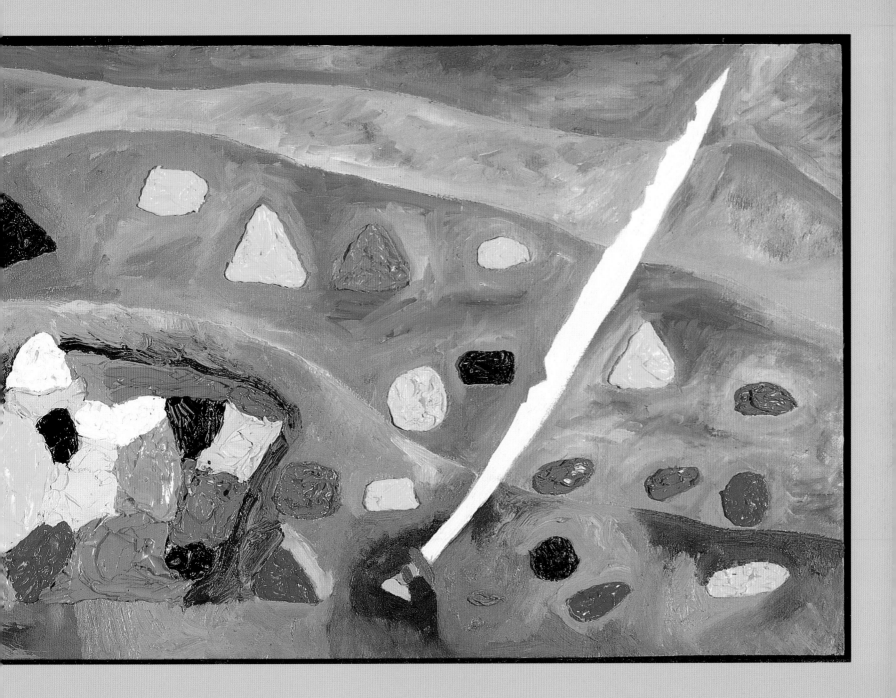

—¡ES UN EMPATE!— dijeron la espada y la piedra y se lloraron las dos de lo inútil de su pelea.

Mientras, estaba el agua del arroyo nomás mirando la pelea y nada decía. La miró la espada y dijo: —¡Tú eres la más débil de todos! Nada puedes hacer a nadie. ¡Yo soy más fuerte que tú!— y se lanzó la espada con grande fuerza contra el agua del arroyo. Un gran escándalo y un ruidero se hizo, se espantaron los peces y el agua no resistió el golpe de la espada.

"'IT'S A DRAW!' said the sword and the stone, and they wept together about how futile their battle had been.

"Meanwhile, the water in the arroyo was watching the fight and saying nothing. The sword looked at the water and said: 'You are the weakest of all! You can't do nothing to anybody. I am stronger than you!' And the sword slashed against the water of the arroyo with great force. The sword made a great big fuss and a lot of noise. The fish got scared, and the water did not resist the sword's blow.

POCO A POCO, sin decir nada, el agua volvió a tomar su forma, a envolver la espada, y a seguir su camino al río que la llevaría al agua grande que hicieron los dioses para curarse la sed que les daba.

"**LITTLE BY LITTLE,** without saying anything, the water took its shape again, wrapping itself around the sword. Then it went on its way to the river that would take it to the big water which the gods had made to cure themselves of their thirst.

PASÓ EL TIEMPO y la espada en el agua se empezó a hacer vieja y oxidada, perdió el filo y los pescados se le acercaban sin miedo y se burlaban de ella. Con pena se retiró la espada del agua del arroyo.

Sin filo ya y derrotada se quejó: Soy más fuerte que ella, pero no le puedo hacer daño y ella a mí, sin pelear, me ha vencido.

"TIME PASSED, and the sword in the water began to grow old and rusty. It lost its edge. The fish would approach it without fear and would mock it. Embarrassed, the sword retreated from the water of the arroyo.

"Without sharpness and defeated, it complained: 'I am stronger than the water, but I cannot harm her. And the water, without fighting, has conquered me.'

SE PASÓ la madrugada y vino el sol a levantar al hombre y a la mujer que se habían cansado juntos para hacerse nuevos. Encontraron el hombre y la mujer a la espada en un rincón oscuro, a la piedra hecha pedacera, al árbol caído y al agua del arroyo cantando…

"ACABARON LOS ABUELOS de contarse la historia de la espada, el árbol, la piedra y el agua y se dijeron:

84

"THE DAWN PASSED and the sun came to wake up the man and the woman who had tired each other to make themselves new. The man and the woman found the sword in a dark corner, the stone broken into pieces, the tree toppled over, and the water of the arroyo singing…

"OUR GRANDFATHERS finished telling each other the story of the sword, the tree, the stone and the water by saying:

85

HAY VECES QUE DEBEMOS PELEAR como si fuéramos espada frente al animal, hay veces que tenemos que pelear como árbol frente a la tormenta, hay veces que tenemos que pelear como piedra frente al tiempo. Pero hay veces que tenemos que pelear como el agua frente a la espada, al árbol y la piedra.

Esta es la hora de hacernos agua y seguir nuestro camino hasta el río que nos lleve al agua grande donde curan su sed los grandes dioses, los que nacieron el mundo, los primeros".

"'THERE ARE TIMES when we must fight as if we are a sword confronted by a wild animal. There are times when we must fight like a tree in the midst of a storm. There are times when we must fight like a stone confronting the elements. But there are times when we must fight like the water fought against the sword.

"'Now is the hour of turning ourselves into water so we can continue on our way toward the river that carries us to the big water where the great gods cure their thirst, the gods that birthed the world, the first gods.'"

Por mi voz habla la voz del Ejército Zapatista de Liberación Nacional

—**ASÍ HICIERON**
nuestros abuelos—
dice el viejo Antonio.
Resistieron como el
agua resiste los golpes
más fieros. Llegó el
extranjero con su
fuerza, espantó a los
débiles, creyó que
ganó y al tiempo se
fue haciendo viejo
y oxidado.

Terminó el extraño
en un rincón lleno de
pena y sin entender
por qué, si ganó,
estaba perdido.

"THIS IS WHAT our grandfathers did," says Old Antonio. "They resisted like the water resists the most savage of blows. The foreigner came here with his power and scared the weak. He thought he had won, but with time he became old and full of rust. The stranger ended up in a corner full of shame and without understanding why, if he had won, he ended up lost."

EL VIEJO ANTONIO vuelve a encender la pipa y la leña del fogón y agrega:

—Así fue como nuestros más grandes y sabios abuelos ganaron la gran guerra al extranjero. El extraño se fue. Nosotros aquí estamos, como el agua del arroyo seguimos caminando al río que habrá de llevarnos al agua grande donde se curan la sed los más grandes dioses, los que nacieron el mundo, los primeros...

OLD ANTONIO once more lights his pipe with the wood of the campfire. And he adds:

"So this was how our greatest and wisest grandfathers won the great war against the foreigner. The stranger left. We are here, and like the water of the arroyo we continue traveling to the river that will take us to the great water where the oldest of gods cure their thirst, those gods that birthed the world, the first ones…"

SE FUE LA MADRUGADA y con ella el viejo Antonio. Yo seguí el camino del sol, a occidente, bordeando un arroyo que serpenteaba hasta el río.

Frente al espejo, entre el sol del amanecer y el sol del atardecer está la tierna caricia del sol de medianoche. Un alivio que es herida. Un agua que es sed. Un encuentro que sigue siendo búsqueda...

DAWN LEFT and so did Old Antonio. I followed the sun's path westward along an arroyo that snaked toward the river.

Facing a mirror, between the morning sun and the setting sun, is the tender caress of the midnight sun—a healing that is a wound, water that is thirst, an encounter that is still a quest...

COMO LA ESPADA del cuento del viejo Antonio, la ofensiva gubernamental de febrero entró sin ninguna dificultad en tierras zapatistas.

Poderosa, deslumbrante, con hermosa empuñadura la espada del Poder golpeó el territorio zapatista.

LIKE THE SWORD in Old Antonio's story, the government's February offensive[8] entered into Zapatista country without difficulty.

Powerful, dazzling, with a beautiful hilt, the Sword of Power slashed at the Zapatista territory.

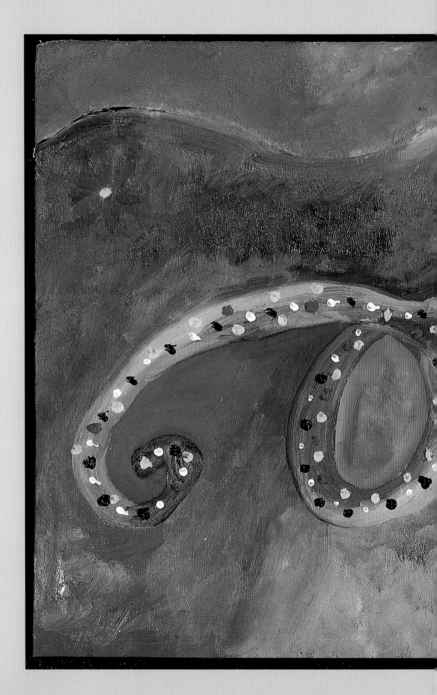

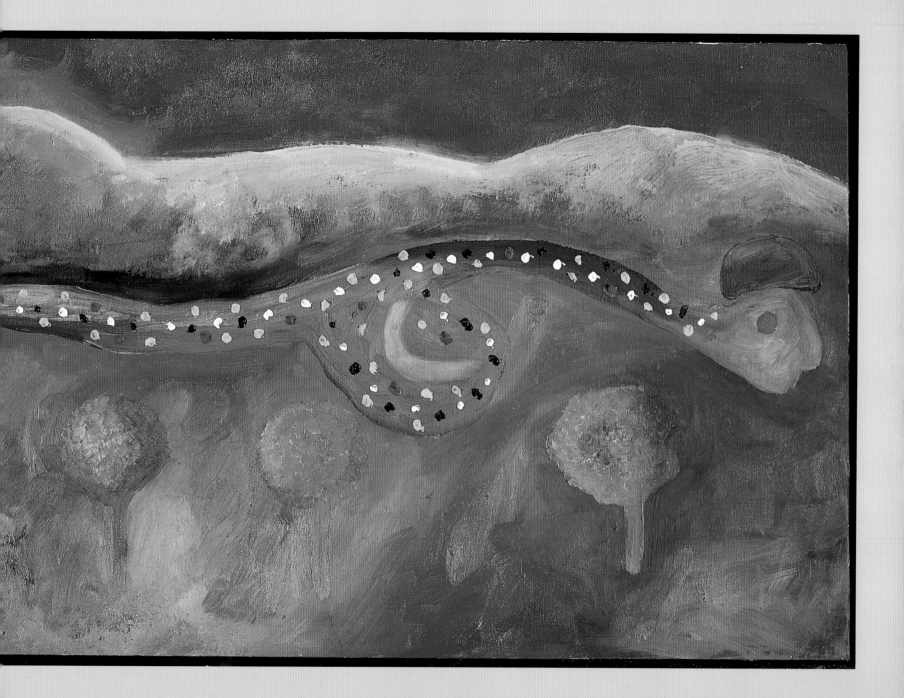

COMO LA ESPADA

del cuento del viejo
Antonio, hizo gran
ruido y escándalo,
como ella, espantó a
algunos peces. Como
en el cuento del viejo
Antonio, su golpe
fue grande, fuerte…
e inútil. Como la
espada del cuento del
viejo Antonio, sigue
en el agua, se oxida
y envejece.

LIKE THE SWORD of Old Antonio's story, the government's offensive made a lot of noise and a big fuss. And it scared some fishes. Like in Old Antonio's story, its blow was big and strong…and useless. Like the sword in Old Antonio's story, it's still in the water, rusting and growing old.

¿EL AGUA? Sigue su camino, envuelve a la espada y, sin hacerle caso, se llega hasta el río que habrá de llevarla hasta el agua grande donde se curan la sed los más grandes dioses, los que nacieron el mundo, los primeros.

THE WATER? It follows its own road. It wraps itself around the sword and, without paying attention, it arrives itself at the river that will carry it to the great water where the greatest of gods cure themselves of thirst, those gods that birthed the world, the first ones.

THE "STORY OF THE SWORD" explains the moral nature of the Zapatista rebellion. In this story, beautifully illustrated by Domitila Domínguez (Domi), Subcomandante Marcos warns us not to practice violence against those who appear weak. He concludes that "we must be like water." It so happens that the sword, a false instrument of power, subjugates the tree and cuts it down. Next, it breaks the stone into pieces, even at the price of dulling its edge. Staring at the calm, meek water, the sword boasts of its invincibility, but the water's quiet presence exasperates it.

Can a book explode like a bomb?

by Elena Poniatowska

Translated by
Aurora Comacho de Schmidt
& Arthur Schmidt

When the sword finally throws itself into the water's arms, it rusts and dies. What the sword could do to the tree and the stone, it could not do to the water. Like Narcissus, the sword dies, drowned in its own reflection.

This is not a story with a moral: it is rather an ethical metaphor. The behavior of the Mexican Army in the indigenous communities of Chiapas has been that of the sword. On January 1, 1994, as the North American Free Trade Agreement was going into effect, the armed movement of the Zapatista Army of National Liberation rose up in the mountains of Mexico's southeast, in Chiapas. The immediate objective of the movement was to protest the implementation of this treaty that would benefit only 10 percent of the Mexican population, forgetting that sixty million Mexicans live in extreme poverty, and many die of curable diseases.

The language of Marcos is the language of a man who has endured life in the jungle for over twenty-five years; a man who has eaten snakes; a college professor (with a big nose, green eyes, a pipe and a beard) who knows many stomach ailments because getting used to the tropics has taken a toll on him. This language is new in Mexican public life and inaugurates a new way of doing politics, one steeped in culture. Marcos rejects the infamous rhetoric of the parties in power. Instead, he uses words that we can all understand, words forged in the long hours spent with the men, women, and children of Chiapas. Sharing these people's living conditions, Marcos knows the sting of the *chechem*, a mos-

quito called "bad woman" that causes a high fever and delirium, and the bite of the *bac Ne'*, the dangerous four-nosed snake. Marcos has walked for days and days in the rain; he can carry a forty-kilo backpack and make headway for hours with no rest; he can tighten his belt and skip meals for several days; he can lead others, but most of all he can think. His words are those of the peasants of Chiapas who through many years of shared life have given him their wisdom. His words are the words of the land; they are the words of survival. Marcos writes under a tree and speaks constantly of his friendship with the beetle Durito, with the setting sun, with the fog that thickens before dawn, with the biting chill, with the star grass, with old Antonio, with Moi, Tacho, Monarca, Ramona, Maribel, Anna María, the crickets, and the grasshoppers.

Marcos, the subcomandante of the indigenous army, demonstrated almost immediately that his understanding of war was uncommon. The fighting lasted twelve days; the Mexican army went as far as bombing some areas. The government responded to the

EZLN offensive with immediate violence and later attempted to eliminate the support that the EZLN had among the peasantry. The international press discovered that Mexico was not a first-world country after all, and the truth of the heroic Zapatistas penetrated deeply into public opinion. Only the demonstrations of students, professors, and housewives in great popular mobilizations were able to stop the genocide. Yielding to pressure, President Carlos Salinas de Gortari offered to pardon the rebels. It was then that Subcomandante Marcos answered with the most impressive of his

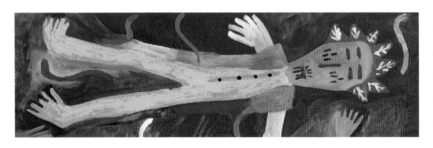

communiqués, one that has journeyed across the oceans and invited responses from the United States, Germany, Canada, Spain, Italy, France, Great Britain, El Salvador, Switzerland, Brazil, Holland, Chile, Norway, Japan, Puerto Rico, Panama, South Africa, Ireland, and Portugal. (In Portugal the man who would eventually win the Nobel Prize, writer José Saramago, supported Zapatismo from the very beginning).

After a first communiqué that used the old jargon of the Stalinist left, Marcos changed the tone of his writing radically, as is dramatically evident in the famous declaration of 1994 to former President Salinas de Gortari, who had offered conditional "pardon" to the insurgents. This statement is considered the best argument in favor of indigenous rights as it asks: "And what are they going to forgive us for? For not dying of hunger? For not keeping quiet in our misery? For not accepting humbly the gigantic historic burden of contempt and abandonment? For rising up in arms when all other roads were closed before us?"

The Zapatista war is a peaceful war, a war of ideas and not of weapons. It aims at defending the indigenous population of the country. This ideology caused *Der Spiegel* in Germany to label Marcos in 1996 "the first postmodern warrior."

In a letter to a child of La Paz, Baja California in March 1994, Marcos wrote:

"At one point we decided to become soldiers so that someday soldiers will no longer be necessary. In other words, we chose a suicidal profession whose objective is to disappear. We are soldiers who are soldiers so that no one else will have to be a soldier. It's all very clear, isn't it?"

The Zapatista rebellion has historical relevance in Mexico and all over Latin America, not only because of Marcos' particular understanding of warfare, but also because the masked men and women of the EZLN placed five hundred years of indigenous repression in the public arena.

The most important claim of the Zapatista movement at this point is to bring to fulfillment the San Andrés Accords, a framework for the defense of indigenous rights. The Accords contain agreements on education, culture, autonomous municipalities, respect for traditions, and health care. The Zapatistas do not want their people to die of curable diseases: measles, whooping cough, dengue fever, cholera, typhoid fever, mono-

nucleosis, tetanus, pneumonia, malaria, and other assorted gas-trointestinal and respiratory afflictions.

The Mexican government has responded with hostility to the Zapatista Movement and its sympathizers all over the world. The national army and the paramilitary groups have invaded indigenous settlements, killing Tzotzil, Tzeltal, Tojolabal, and Chontal people. In December of 1997, in the highland town of Acteal, paramilitaries fired upon 45 villagers while they prayed in a small chapel. The assailants followed those who fled down the ravine and hacked them to death. Most of the victims were women and children.

The administration of President Ernesto Zedillo failed to implement the San Andrés Accords, which it signed. Zedillo betrayed the indigenous negotiators, just as he and his predecessor Salinas de Gortari betrayed the causes of the poorest Mexicans.

The Zapatista army created a civilian consciousness, not only among the students who collect food, clothing, and money and organize caravans to Chiapas, but also among a previously indifferent population that now supports the EZLN from the Federal District, many other cities of the Mexican Republic, the United States, and Europe. In this struggle, the internet plays an essential role for Marcos, the communicator from deep in the jungle. The internet has become a far more efficient tool than a gun; it helps to forestall greater tragedies. The world had never seen or heard a guerrilla on the internet. Che Guevara never possessed such a wide-reaching instrument. Subcomandante Marcos communicates with the rest of the world in a blink of an eye. The Zapatista struggle is a war of sorts that has evoked massive national and international responses. If the Mexican government dared to eliminate Marcos and the Zapatistas, it would undoubtedly face immediate international condemnation.

The Zapatistas in the mountains of Mexico's southeast are part of the universe. Their cry crosses the air on the wings of the internet, reaching five continents. Durito navigates on a can of sardines like an admiral on the ocean sea, reaching the coasts of Italy, Holland, and Spain. The green, sagacious, and mischievous eyes of Subcomandante Marcos travel over the waves of the Atlantic and Pacific, coming ashore all over the world. In the same global fashion, Domitila Domínguez drapes over us the "green lightening of parrots"—reminding us of Ramón López Velarde, our poet from Zacatecas—and "the blue storm that falls under the weight of its purpleness," as our poet from Tabasco, Carlos Pellicer, would have said it. The canyons descend to the bottom of the earth and traverse it until they reach other towns, colorful and fraternal. This is why we know that we will rise again, and we will be forest, water, beetles (although not as wise as Durito, of course), pipes, smoke, chimneys, smog, ashes, and yes, dust, but dust-in-love. With colorful dust, Domi illustrates the fable of the sword.

Domi paints to celebrate life, death, the cornfield, the rambling vine, the sunset, the water, and the gods. There are those who tell her that all the indigenous wisdom is concentrated in her work, and that her fingers, as they paint the earth, return to us

bathed in colors what was before only gray and black, like our own routines, or like the ski masks of the Zapatista insurgents in the jungle of Chiapas.

Everything comes out of the fog, and everything goes back to the fog, but Domi's brush strokes are strong, and so are her colors. No pastel colors for her, or little dolls dressed in blue. Here any gaze is rotund, and the stroke of a brush is like the trajectory of a bullet. (Have you ever noticed that weapons have no color?) Domi loves little red, yellow and white dots, and with her brush she sprinkles fishes and tigers, turtles, horses, and cows. The dot is a seed, and any well-planted seed can contain all the love in the world. The dot, as Domi knows so well, is the roundness of the earth, the grain in the furrow, and the end of the story.

Can a book explode like a bomb? Can it change minds? Should a government feel threatened? Do books bite and make others rabid? The Subcomandante and Domitila Domínguez trust in the power of books. She illustrated *The Story of Colors/ La historia de los colores* (published by Cinco Puntos Press) and was thus sealed with the fire of a struggle in which ski masks are popular art. The imagination of Marcos and Domitila give them powers to discover why we are here. To follow them is not only a step toward knowledge, it is also a way of breaking limits— political, social or cultural—and perceiving the moral dimension of our lives.

Naturally, Marcos' words would not have had the same effect had he not been a writer and had his political discourse not been also a poetic discourse. He could have spoken as one more leftist; instead he translated the indigenous way of feeling. He shed his urban upbringing, his city ways, and grew up again side by side with beetles, indigenous children and women, old wizards, birds and

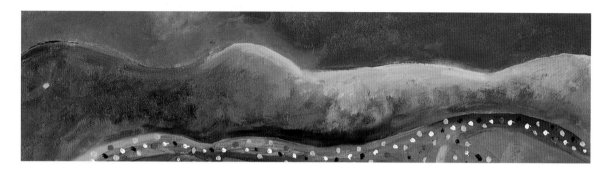

trees. Flowers grew on top of his head (you can see them if you remove his khaki cap), and he acquired a new knowledge. He is already a great tree among trees, his freshness and anti-solemnity break with the fundamentalist left; this combination puts the government and the official politicians in check. None of them could have ever pronounced Marcos' words: "Who can ask for pardon and who can give it?" Marcos fights with words. His weapon is his pen.

Chiapas is a very rich region that produces petroleum, coffee, bananas and cocoa. Potentially it could supply water to the entire Mexican Republic. And yet the poorest and most abandoned of all Mexicans survive there under inhuman conditions. Marcos tells the story of Toñita, the six-year-old girl who fled her home to hide in the mountains with a pair of white shoes, new and shiny, a gift from a kind person. She was carrying them in her hands. "Why don't you put them on?" Marcos asked. "Cause they'll get muddy," she answered. So that this little girl will be able to wear her shoes, so that the dignity of the indigenous people of Chiapas will be respected, so that the popular heroes Villa and Zapata will acquire a new meaning, the EZLN continues fighting for the smallest ones who even today, five hundred years later, have neither land nor freedom, nor a roof over their heads, nor work, nor health care, nor food, nor education, nor opportunities.

Article 39 of our constitution says that any public power derives from the people and is instituted for their benefit, and that at any time the people have the inalienable right to alter or to modify their form of government.

Chiapas is now a tangible nightmare in which the fury of power is poured against indigenous human beings. The EZLN, and Marcos as its interpreter, rise to tell us that as the sword rusts in the water, it becomes useless and loses its purpose. And they tell us with the voice of the rain and the waterfall that in Chiapas there is much water.

—*Elena Poniatowska*

ELENA PONIATOWSKA, *one of Mexico's most respected writers, is a journalist, novelist and poet. Born in Paris, France of Polish and Mexican parents, Elena has lived in Mexico since 1942, becoming a citizen in 1969. Her many books and articles have long announced the fact that she is a spokesperson for human rights and dignity for all peoples. Since January 1, 1994, she has been an advocate for the causes of the EZLN, interviewing Marcos on various occasions. Her latest novel,* La piel del cielo, *received the prestigious Premio Alfaguara de Novela 2001.*

ANTONIO RAMÍREZ was born in 1944 in Mexico City, the youngest of nine children in a working class family. He had to quit school to work, but at age 14 he enrolled in the National School of Painting and Sculpture ("La Esmeralda"), where he studied at night. When he turned 17, he left home and traveled toward the southeast of Mexico, working in the village of Arroyo León, in Veracrúz, teaching children and adults to read and write. There he saw with his own eyes the injustices and humiliation suffered by poor campesinos and native peoples.

The people of Arroyo León went shopping each week in a nearby village named Nuevo Ixcatlán, an indigenous Mazatecan community. That's where Antonio met Domitila. Domi had been born in a neighboring town, but when she was five, the Mexican government relocated her parents—along with more than half of their pueblo—to accommodate the construction of a dam. From early childhood, Domi had enjoyed watching her aunts create the patterns and embroider the cloth to make huipiles, the loose brocaded blouses worn by Mayan women. She remembers sitting by the door of her family's hut and embroidering little blankets with many-colored threads. When Domi first met Antonio and saw the fantastical animals and equally fantastical humans and flowers in his paintings, she became encouraged to do the same thing in her embroidery.

Before she turned 15, she began living with Antonio. They began to move where they could find work, hiring out in factories and workshops and doing their art at night. In 1967, they were living in Mexico City where they participated in the marches and meetings that led up to the populist Student Movement of 1968. The immediate outcome of that movement was tragedy. Ordaz-Diaz, the president of Mexico, in order to save face before the 1968 Olympics, ordered the Mexican Army to disband the students. The result was the slaughter in the Plaza of Three Cultures of Tlatelolco. The Mexican police killed hundreds of students and supporters, washed away the blood and lied about the casualties. The U.S. government and the media ignored the massacre. A few days later the Olympics began to much fanfare, and soon international news concentrated on Americans Tommie Smith and John Carlos, who finished 1-3 in the 200-meter run—they

IN 1985, artists Antonio Ramirez and Domitila (Domi) Domínquez, along with like-minded artist friends and members of their family, formed the Colectivo Callejero, "the streetwise collective." The group is dedicated to expressing through art the political thought of the left in Mexico— in particular, as it concerns the struggles of indigenous peoples. This is the story of how the Colectivo came into being.

El Colectivo Callejero

bowed their heads and gave the Black Power salute during the national anthem as a protest against racism in the U.S.

Brutal repression became the rule of Mexico. Like many of their contemporaries, Antonio and Domi moved away from Mexico City. They continued to piece together a living while working intensely with other leftist artists who were looking for ways to dovetail their art and politics. They participated actively in supporting tenants' and squatters' organizations, and they created, either collectively or as individuals, numerous political street murals and anti-capitalist pamphlets which criticized the government and the compromising left.

But during these intense and difficult times, Domi and Antonio also established themselves truly as a family. They had four children, all of whom still have close ties with their parents and participate, in one way or another, in the ideas and projects of the Colectivo Callejero.

In 1983 the family moved to Guadalajara where they now live. It was here that two important transitions occurred. First, Antonio was finally able to work exclusively as an artist instead of dividing his time between art and the jobs required for the livelihood of their family. Also, shortly after their arrival in Guadalajara, Domi realized that painting came effortlessly for her. Since then her work has grown with total naturalness and fluidity— in etching and sculpture as well as in painting.

In 1985, a group of friends—Antonio and Domi among them—conceived the idea of creating a collective portfolio of serigraphs with the issues of urban life being the unifying theme. For them the politics of the left suffered from the absence of a hugely important ingredient—the artistic element. It had no ambiente. No soul. They wanted to create work that reached out to everyday men and women, people on the street. They named themselves el Colectivo Callejero— "the streetwise collective." They opened an alternative cultural center in Guadalajara which they named la Grieta, "The Crack." The purpose of the center was not to advertise the work of its founders, but to promote an alternative art scene which had political and aesthetic principles similar to those of the Colectivo Callejero. Although short-lived, la Grieta was the focus of intense artistic and intellectual activity, and a major turning point in the understanding of its founders.

In 1988, the Colectivo Callejero published a series of seven serigraphed posters, each poster created by a different member of the Colectivo. The posters recalled the 20 years of the student movement, "1968–1988: There is Memory." They produced 3,500 full-color posters of each serigraph, and pasted them on the walls of busy streets and thoroughfares in Mexico City and Guadalajara. This was guerrilla art—profitless, nameless and destined to be destroyed.

When the EZLN marched out of the Lacandón jungle and declared war against the Mexican government on the first of January 1994, the Colectivo Callejero immediately identified themselves with the Indian rebels' struggle. Since then, the Colectivo has centered its activities on supporting the words and deeds of the Zapatistas with artistic images. Their primary project has been a series of books that illustrated the words of Subcomandante Marcos, in particular the stories of el viejo Antonio. Among these were *The Story of Colors / La Historia de los Colores*, re-published by Cinco Puntos in 1998, and the two stories included in this book.

Domi's numerous paintings, reproduced profusely in books and calendars, have contributed greatly to a wider understanding of the struggles of indigenous people in Mexico. In 1995, as recognition of her work, the EZLN invited Domi to serve as an advisor to the dialogs at San Andrés.

In 2000, working on a large commission from the University of Guadalajara in the Jalisco city of Zapotlán el Grande, Antonio completed a mural al fresco "The Dream and Nightmare of Power." The mural, which measures 135 square meters, pays homage to the Zapatista movement in Chiapas.

Below is a brief list of readily available resources for readers in English who want to know more about the EZLN.

The War Against Oblivion: Zapatista Chronicles 1994 – 2000, by John Ross. Common Courage Press, 2000.

Our Word is Our Weapon: Selected Writings by Subcomandante Insurgente Marcos. Edited by Juana Ponce de Leon. Seven Stories Press, 2000.

The Story of Colors / La Historia de los Colores, A Folktale from the Jungles of Chiapas, by Subcomandante Insurgente Marcos. Illustrated by Domitila Domínguez. Cinco Puntos Press, 1998.

www.ezln.org This indispensable website archives in English and Spanish all of Marcos' communiqués, as well as providing current EZLN news, links to other sources and a variety of other information.

Notes

1. **TRANSLATOR'S STATEMENT**.

I asked my Mexico City friends—all of them admirers of Marcos and his writing—if they had any ideas about how to translate these stories into English. They just shook their heads. "It's such bad Spanish," they said. Marcos certainly knows it's "bad Spanish." But he's trying to replicate the Spanish Viejo Ántonio speaks—the way indigenous people of Chiapas speak Spanish. It's their Spanish, the way that the indigenous languages and syntax regurgitate Spanish orally. In "The Story of Questions" especially ("The Sword" is more measured and dignified), the Spanish has a folksy, somewhat iconoclastic humor. The way the words and syntax get skewered reminds me of the great Mexican comic Cantinflas—with his hilarious ramblings that were childlike, obscure and wise all at once.

Viejo Antonio's purpose is mostly serious, of course, but we get the sense that for him the sacred and the comical aren't that far apart. It's almost impossible to translate the zaniness of Viejo Antonio's speech patterns into English. I briefly considered having Viejo Antonio speak a kind of Black English or even a border "Spanglish." This would approximate the "ungrammatical" zest of his manner of talking. But these solutions would have created other problems. Overall, it is easier to capture the wisdom and poetry of Viejo Antonio's language than it is the underlying sharp-witted sense of humor. But hopefully there are some rhythms in this English translation, especially when reading it aloud, where there's an echo of that.

Marcos himself found out the hard way about that Indian sense of humor. He learned to speak four Mayan languages, he once told a reporter, to protect himself against their laughter. While working as a community organizer during the early '80s in the jungle villages of Chiapas, he'd run into Indians who would "start saying all sorts of crap about me. They would just start laughing in front of me, making fun of me, and it was real tough not knowing what they were saying." So he learned the Chol, Tzeltal, Tzotzil and Tojolabal languages to defend himself. "The first thing you gotta learn are the cuss words," the guerilla leader explained, "for survival's sake."

Since then, Marcos has learned not only the words but also the worldviews, lifeways and stories belonging to those Mayan communities, but, more important to us, he has learned to translate these indigenous ideas to the world community. In fact, part of what has made the guerilla leader so effective in reaching a post-modern, wired-together world is that he's one hell of a translator.

—*DAVID ROMO*

2. December 13, 1994—Ernesto Zedillo was the new president of Mexico; the peso and the Mexican economy were on the verge of collapse; and the EZLN, certain that the Mexican government was about to attack, were preparing to disappear into the jungle.

3. *1984*. Marcos and the EZLN seemed to be measuring time before and after January 1, 1994, the day the EZLN woke up the world by marching out of the Lacandón Jungle and occupying San Cristobal de las Casas.

4. In 1910, *Anenecuilco,* a small village of 400 in Morelos, elected 30-year-old Emiliano Zapata as head of its council. His responsibility was to defend the community's existing land and water rights and to win back communal land taken by rich farmers. The following year, after Francisco Madero had been installed as the first post-Porfirio Diaz president of Mexico, he dispatched General Victoriano Huerta against the "bandits" of Morelos. Zapata reorganized his army to meet the challenge, and on November 25, 1911 he issued his famous *Plan de Ayala* in which he denounced Madero: "We again take up [arms] against him for defaulting on the promises of the Mexican people and for betraying the Revolution initiated by him. We are not personalists; we are partisans of principles and not of men." On April 10, 1919, Colonel Jesús Guajardo, feigning defection to Zapata's side, invited the rebel leader into the *Chinameca* hacienda for beer and a meal. As he and his 10-man escort rode through the hacienda's gates, gunfire rained down on them. Zapata died instantly.

5. September 29, 1995—during the 18-month negotiations between the government and the EZLN that resulted in the San Andres Accord. "The Story of the Sword" is a postscript to a communiqué in which Marcos reports on the Zapatista "consultation," a national and international popular plebiscite organized to allow Mexicans and others to demonstrate their solidarity with the EZLN.

6. On September 19, 1985, at 7:17 A.M., a Richter magnitude 8.1 earthquake rumbled through Mexico City. Of a population of 18 million, the quake killed an estimated 10,000 people and injured 50,000. In addition, 250,000 people lost their homes, and over 800 buildings crumbled, including hotels, hospitals, schools and businesses.

7. The War of Independence from Spain began on September 16, 1810, when Miguel Hidalgo y Costilla, a parish priest in Dolores, climbed into his pulpit and proclaimed, among other statements, "Long live Mexico!" This is "El Grito," the shout of Mexican Independence. The names that follow are all heroes of that 10-year war.

8. On February 9, 1995—when the peso was at its all-time low against the dollar, Mexico was experiencing its worse depression since 1932, and the U.S. was sending in emergency Clinton-blessed loans—Ernesto Zedillo dispatched thousands of troops into the mountains of Chiapas to capture EZLN leadership. Marcos and the Zapatistas escaped into the treacherous terrain of the Blue Mountains.